This book belongs to:

....

....

For Mom and Dad, with all my love

Sandy Creek
NEW YORK

An Imprint of Sterling Publishing Co., Inc.
1166 Avenue of the Americas
New York, NY 10036

Text © 2013 by QEB Publishing, Inc.
Illustrations © 2013 by QEB Publishing, Inc.

ISBN 978-1-4351-5602-9

Manufactured in Guangdong, China
Lot #:
2 4 6 8 10 9 7 5 3
06/16

www.sterlingpublishing.com

Editor: Ruth Symons
Designer: Bianca Lucas
Managing Editor: Victoria Garrard
Design Manager: Anna Lubecka

SQUIRREL'S BUSY DAY

by Lucy Barnard

Sandy Creek
NEW YORK

It was fall, so Squirrel decided
to spend the day collecting acorns.

He set off down the path with his old red wagon.

Squirrel hadn't gone far when
Rabbit bounced out of the bushes.

"Morning, Squirrel!" Rabbit said.
"Do you want to play tag
through the leaves?"

"I can't today,
I'm too busy,"
Squirrel said,
and he hurried along.

Soon, Squirrel met his friend Mouse.

"Do you want to come and play in my nest?" squeaked Mouse.

"Not right now, I don't have time," Squirrel said, and he rushed off.

Squirrel had lots of acorns
in his wagon when he
passed Badger's den.

"Hello, Squirrel," Badger called out.
"How are you today?"

"No time to talk, I'm gathering acorns!"
Squirrel said, and he scurried away.

Squirrel's wagon was nearly full when he met Owl and Fox.

"HelloOOOOO, Squirrel," hooted Owl.

"It's a lovely day," barked Fox. "Come and play!"

"I don't have time today, I'm in a hurry," puffed Squirrel, tugging at his wagon.

Huff! Puff!

At last,
Squirrel's wagon was full —
and very, very heavy.

As he heaved it to the top of
a steep hill, he heard a loud...

CRACK!

The handle had
**snapped
off!**

The broken wagon
rolled down the hill,
hit a stone and...

CRASH!

The acorns went flying.

Just then the leaves behind Squirrel rustled.

"I heard
a noise,"
hooted Owl.

"Are you okay?"
Fox asked.

"My acorns have gone everywhere,"
Squirrel said. "I'll never find them all!"

"We'll help you," squeaked Mouse.
"Together, we'll find them in no time."

And that's just what they did...

Mouse found **one** under a big leaf.

Fox found **two** beside some mushrooms.

Owl found **three** in a group of pinecones.

Badger found
four behind
a mossy log.

And Rabbit found
five on some
pointy grass.

The animals piled all the acorns into the wagon.

Then they helped Squirrel push the wagon back home.

"I'm sorry I didn't stop to play,"
Squirrel said. "You've all been so kind."

"That's what friends are for!"
Badger replied with a smile.

"Friends are also for playing
tag with," laughed Squirrel,
as he raced off through the leaves.

"Catch me if you can!"

NEXT STEPS

Show the children the cover again. Could they have guessed what the story is about? Does the title give them a clue?

When you have read the story together, ask the children why Squirrel was too busy to play with his friends. Why do they think Squirrel was collecting so many acorns?

Squirrel was too busy to spend time with his friends, but they helped him when he needed them. Working together, the animals found all of the acorns. Ask the children about their friends. When have they helped a friend?

Talk to the children about the other characters in the story. Have they ever seen those animals before? Ask the children to draw their favorite animal from the story.

Act out the story. Perhaps one of the children could collect balls, toys, or balloons instead of acorns. Do any of them have a cart or a wagon like Squirrel's?

At the end of the story, the animals play tag. What games do the children like to play with their friends?